DRAGLINS
AND THE
BULLY!

WITHDRAWN

VIVIAN FRENCH   CHRIS FISHER

ORCHARD BOOKS

CHAPTER ONE

"SCHOOL? US? Go to SCHOOL?" Daffodil stared at Aunt Plum as if she had suggested her four nieces and nephews cut their own tails off.

Aunt Plum sighed. She had suspected Daffodil would be difficult. "Daffodil dear," she explained for the tenth time, "the uncles and I have decided it just isn't safe for you and Dora and Dennis and Danny to run wild out here. You were all brought up in the warmth and safety of Under Roof, and you don't realise how dangerous Outdoors can be."

Daffodil snorted loudly. "I can take care of myself," she said. "And so can Dennis and Danny. Send Dora to school. She'd love it!" Daffodil paused. If nothing else, she was fair. "Actually, Aunt Plum, Dora's pretty good at adventures. When she met that chat—"

5

"DAFFODIL!" Aunt Plum said sharply. "You're not listening to me! All four of you are going to go to school, and you're going to start tomorrow. And Pip is going to go to nursery, so you can take him with you." She sighed. "It'll give me the chance to give Under Shed a really good spring-clean. Your uncles are very fine draglins, but they are NOT tidy, and having all of us living here as well makes things ten times worse. Now, go and make the most of today. Uncle Puddle's going to take you to school at nine o'clock tomorrow morning – and that's the end of it. So no more arguing!"

As Aunt Plum trotted away into the kitchen Daffodil frowned horribly, and went to call a council of war. She found Dennis, Danny and Dora playing with Pip on the swing behind the uncles' house, and stormed over to tell them the dreadful news.

The area the draglins called Under Shed

6

was surprisingly large. Many years before, Human Beanies had built a wooden shed at the bottom of a row of shared gardens, and although the shed itself was now in ruins, the floor provided a splendidly solid roof for the uncles' house. There was also a huge storage space behind the house (much cluttered with the uncles' collections of Useful Things), and a safe place for the draglins to play.

Just the week before Uncle Plant had

rigged up a swing, and Pip happily spent hours swinging to and fro.

"Honestly!" Daffodil began, "you'd think we were BABIES the way Aunt Plum treats us! Do you know what she's done now?"

"She's sending us to school," Dora said. She tried not to look pleased. School meant a nice safe everyday life – and hopefully no adventures.

Danny nodded. "She told us earlier. It'll be OK. I'm quite looking forward to it, actually."

"It'll be great!" Dennis gave Pip a mighty push, and the little draglin squealed with excitement as he soared into the air. "We'll meet LOADS of other draglins! Uncle Plant says there's a bootball team, and all kinds of other stuff!"

Daffodil stared angrily at them. This was not at all the reaction she had expected. "Well, I'M not going!" she declared. "I can take care of myself, and I told Aunt Plum I could, so there!"

"You'll get really fed up hanging around here all day by yourself," Danny said in an irritatingly reasonable way. "You'll probably have to spend all the time looking after Pip."

"He's going to go to nursery," Daffodil told him. "Aunt Plum says she's going to spring clean Under Shed while we're out."

Dennis shuddered. "I'd MUCH rather be at school than be here while she's doing that," he said. "Don't you remember how horrible it was when she did cleaning in Under Roof?"

Daffodil did, and she became suddenly thoughtful. Aunt Plum was an entirely different sort of draglin when on a cleaning mission. Nothing stood in her way, particularly little draglins.

When they had lived in Under Roof at the top of the old tenement the annual spring clean had been a time of total misery while Aunt Plum dusted, mopped and polished.

There they had had to put up with it; now they had moved to the magical world of Outdoors, things were different.

"All right," Daffodil said. "I'll go to school, but only until Aunt Plum's finished."

CHAPTER TWO

Uncle Puddle looked at his nephews and nieces and grinned. Aunt Plum had begun her cleaning early; they were all spotless and, in Danny's case, still rather damp around the neck. Daffodil was inclined to glower; luckily she was a little in awe of Uncle Puddle, so he was spared the grumbling Aunt Plum had had to put up with all through breakfast.

"Right," he said, "have you all got your lunchboxes?" His nephews and nieces nodded. "Good. Dora, you look after Pip on the way to school and take him into nursery. Daffodil, you collect him. Now, I'll be taking you there, but you'll find your own way home. I'm off Collecting later today."

Daffodil visibly brightened. "Cool," she remarked.

Uncle Puddle fixed her with a stern gaze. "School finishes at three," he said. "If you're not back here by half past three at the latest, you'll be in trouble."

Daffodil opened her mouth to argue, then thought better of it. "OK," she said.

The four little draglins and baby Pip lined up behind Uncle Puddle.

"Go and swing?" Pip asked hopefully.

"NO." Daffodil made a face at him. "Horrible horrible SCHOOL!"

Pip began to cry.

"Honestly, Daffy," Dora said crossly as she mopped Pip's tears. "Can't you ever think of anyone except yourself?"

"Sorry." Daffodil fished in her lunchbox, and gave Pip a biscuit. "LOVELY school for Pip!"

Pip sniffed. "Want swing," he muttered, but he stopped crying.

Uncle Puddle ignored the interruption. "We're going through the Underground, of course," he said. "Make sure you check VERY carefully when you're travelling Outdoors. The dangerous bit is the gap between the entrance and our front door."

"Yes, Uncle Puddle," Dora said politely. She was hoping her uncle couldn't hear Daffodil muttering "Yadda yadda yadda", and Dennis making horribly bored yawning noises.

Aunt Plum appeared, her head tied up in a duster. "Is the mud slide still there, Puddle dear?" she asked.

"WHAT mud slide?" Dennis asked.

"Is it a BIG one?" Daffodil's eyes were shining.

Uncle Puddle looked at his quivering nephew and niece. "It's just about dried up," he said, "and we've put a bridge over it." He turned to Danny and Dora. "It's where we used to get clay for making pots and bowls," he explained. "It's more of a clay pit than a mud slide."

"Oh." Daffodil lost interest at once, and Dennis drooped.

"If you're very lucky, you might get to make some lovely coil pots in handicraft," said Aunt Plum.

Daffodil snorted loudly.

"Time to be off!" Uncle Puddle said.

Compared to the Underground journey the draglins had made when they moved from Under Roof to the uncles' house, school was only a short way away.

Daffodil noted the fact with gloom, Dora with pleasure. Danny and Dennis were much too busy discussing what bootball would be like to have any thoughts about the journey, although they paused for a moment when the tunnel narrowed, and they trotted across a small wooden bridge.

Underneath was the clay pit; it wasn't much more than a hollow in the ground, but the yellow clay gleamed stickily in the faint light.

"Be careful when you're coming home," Uncle Puddle said. "We don't want you slipping in here. It's not at all deep, but you'd get your shoes messy, and I can tell you now that your aunt would NOT be happy about that!"

Dora took a firmer grip on Pip's hand. Dennis gave Daffodil a friendly shove. "Saved your life!" he said cheerfully as she staggered, and he pulled her back by her arm.

Uncle Puddle glared at him. "That is NOT funny, Dennis."

"Sorry," Dennis said, and went back to talk bootball tactics with Danny.

Daffodil trailed behind them, a thoughtful expression on her face.

CHAPTER THREE

When they reached a large airy cavern, and Uncle Puddle stopped, they looked round in surprise.

"Here we are," Uncle Puddle said. "This was a burrowing long ago. That's why the school's called Wabbit End. You'll see the main entrance is over there. Be good!"

Daffodil sighed heavily.

"Come on, Daffy-dilly," Danny said encouragingly. "You might enjoy it!"

Daffodil looked at the long low wooden building tucked into the wall of the rabbit burrow. She had decided she was going to hate every minute, and she wasn't going to change her mind now. School! What could they teach that she didn't know? She scowled, and as Danny followed Dennis, Dora and Pip, she dragged behind, scuffing her shoes in the sandy floor.

A bespectacled draglin in a bright flowery dress met the four little draglins and Pip in the hallway. "Good morning!" she said. "You must be the new boys and girls! I'm Mrs Gage, your teacher. And what a dear little fellow this is. Is he your cousin Pip?"

Dora nodded. In all of her short life the only grown-up draglins she had ever met were her uncles and Aunt Plum, and she was suddenly overcome with shyness.

"The nursery's through the classroom, dear," Mrs Gage told her. "If you walk past the desks you'll see the door at the bottom. Settle him down, and come back when you think he's all right. We do want him to be happy here – I always say we're just like one big happy family!"

Daffodil saw an opportunity. "I'll take Pip," she offered. "I don't mind sitting with him."

Mrs Gage eyed Daffodil with interest. "You must be Daffodil," she said. "Your auntie has told me all about you. I hear you have SUCH exciting ideas! We'll let Dora take Pip, shall we? And you can follow me to the classroom. I'll introduce you to Peg. You'll be sitting next to her, and I'm sure you two will be GREAT friends."

Daffodil immediately promised herself that she would never ever be friends with Peg, but she said nothing as Mrs Gage shooed the draglins through a door and into the classroom.

The seven young draglins sitting at their desks stared as Dora, blushing from head to toe, hurried past them with Pip in her arms. She had picked him up more to comfort herself than to make him feel safe, and he was wriggling wildly.

"Down!" he shouted in his squeaky little voice. "Down!"

Dora blushed an even deeper red and scuttled towards the nursery.

Pip began to squirm like an eel, and Dora was forced to drop him. His flailing legs and arms knocked over an enormous bottle of black ink on the largest boy draglin's desk, and the bottle crashed onto the floor, splattering ink in every direction.

"Oi!" said the draglin angrily. "Look what you've done to my bootball boots!"

Dora was so flustered she didn't know what to do. "Sorry!" she said, "I'm very very sorry!" and she grabbed Pip and shot through the nursery door, leaving an ever widening pool of ink behind her.

A furious roar followed her as she arrived panting in the nursery, and a large and comfortable draglin grandmother tut tutted at her crossly.

CHAPTER FOUR

Back in the classroom Mrs Gage bustled into action. "Kittle! Fetch some cloths, sweetie!" she ordered. "Plotter dear – could you fetch some as well? Slump – do please stop shouting, and bring your boots here so I can wipe them. Button and Sam, hurry and move your desks away from the ink."

There was a clattering and thumping as desks were hauled across the floor. Under cover of the racket Peg, who was as wide as she was high, trod heavily on Daffodil's foot and growled, "Roofie! Roofie! Roofie babies don't know NOTHING!" Daffodil dug her sharp little elbow into Peg's solid side, and Peg doubled over, gasping and wailing loudly.

"SILENCE!" yelled Mrs Gage. "SILENCE! Or there'll be a detention!"

Everyone fell silent, except the wailing Peg.

"Goodness me, Peg," Mrs Gage said, "whatever is the matter?"

"She HURT me." Peg pointed at Daffodil.

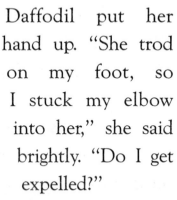

Daffodil put her hand up. "She trod on my foot, so I stuck my elbow into her," she said brightly. "Do I get expelled?"

"Thank you for telling me, Daffodil dear," said Mrs Gage, "but I don't think that will be quite necessary. Just sit down, both of you. Peg, show Daffodil where we are in our reading books."

"What about my boots, Miss?" Slump asked. "They still look messy."

Mrs Gage smiled. "I don't think a little ink will spoil your bootballing skills, Slump.

30

We'll have an early break, and you can show the new boys and girls how good you are at kicking goals."

A slow grin spread across Slump's large face. "Cheers, Miss," he said, and picked up his book.

In the nursery Pip settled down quickly. As Dora walked away, he began happily patting at a lump of clay, and didn't even wave goodbye.

Dora opened the door to the classroom, and peered round. Apart from a nasty black stain on the floor there was no sign of the accident, and Danny, Dennis and Daffodil were sitting at desks as if they'd been in school for ever.

"Ah! There you are, Dora dear," Mrs Gage greeted her. "Is your little cousin happy now?"

Dora nodded. "Yes, thank you. He's playing with the clay."

"Excellent! Perhaps you'd like to sit with Violet?" Mrs Gage pointed to a small and anxious looking draglin at the back of the class. Violet gave Dora a nervous smile and dropped her reading book. Dora's heart leapt as she recognised a soul mate. She squeezed her way between the desks, and sat down.

"I do hope we can be friends," Violet whispered. "Kittle and Button are best friends, and the boys like playing bootball all the time, and Peg doesn't like anyone, so I get left out." She looked sideways at Dora. "And I'm scared of things, so they tease me."

Dora beamed at Violet. "I'm always scared of EVERYTHING," she said.

"Oh, GOOD!" Violet's eyes shone.

"No talking!" Mrs Gage said. "Dora dear, would you like to begin reading?"

The book was full of pictures of cats and dogs, and squirrels and rabbits and birds, and Dora recognised it at once. She was so surprised she spoke without thinking. "I've read this!" she said. "The chats and the dawgs are SCARY!"

There was a loud whisper. "Show-off know-it-all roofie!"

Dora looked up. "I...I didn't mean to show off," she apologised.

Mrs Gage frowned. "Peg," she enquired, "did you just tell Dora she was a show-off?"

"She didn't say anything," Dora said anxiously. "I was – I was just explaining." She hurriedly opened the book, and began to read.

CHAPTER FIVE

B y the time every draglin had had a chance to struggle through a few pages it was break time.

Violet seized Dora's hand as soon as the bell went, and dragged her out into the yard. "Come and play skipping with me," she said. "I've never had a friend to skip with!"

"No skipping," said a booming voice. "You heard what Miss said! You're all going to watch me play bootball!" Slump was grinning hugely, and clutching a blue and white striped ball under his arm.

Peg's large hand grabbed Dora by the shoulder. "That's right! And YOU'RE going to be goalie, 'cos it was you that spoilt Slump's boots!"

Dora went pale. "But I don't know anything about bootball!" she gasped.

Daffodil pushed in front of Dora. "I'LL be goalie!" she announced. "You leave my sister alone, you big bully!"

Peg folded her arms. "Says who?"

"Oh Daffy, DON'T—" Dora began, but it was too late.

"Says ME!" Daffodil said, and she squared up to Peg, her eyes flashing and her fists clenched.

"Hang on a mo, you lot," Slump said. "I never said anything about a goalie…"

Dennis appeared from nowhere, and took his place beside Daffodil. "Trouble!" he said happily. "Count me in! Come on, Danny!"

Danny sighed, and shook his head. "Can't we just watch Slump play bootball?" he asked.

"Yeah!" said Slump.

"NO!" Peg pointed a large finger at Daffodil. "She called me a bully! I'm not having it!"

"You ARE a bully," Daffodil said, and danced up and down in front of Peg.

At the same moment Violet gave a piercing scream. "WABBIT!"

And the world went dark.

39

CHAPTER SIX

Dennis, Danny, Dora and Daffodil were taken completely by surprise, but Kittle, Button and Plotter flew back to the school, and seconds later a candle lit the gloom.

Slump scooped up Dennis and Daffodil and hauled them along with him, and Danny grabbed Dora. Peg thundered behind them, and as they arrived in a heap on the doorstep an elderly rabbit squeezed his way out of the tunnel that led to Wabbit End from the world outside.

As his furry body popped out of the hole, light flooded back. He lolloped across the playground and sat down on the sandy floor, a puzzled expression on his face.

"WOW!" Daffodil said, her eyes wide. "I've never seen a real live wabbit before! It's HUGE!"

Dora was trembling, and very pale. "Will it eat us?" she whispered. "Will it eat us?"

"No way," Slump said. He patted Dora on the back. "Wabbits won't hurt you. Look – even the nursery class is watching!"

Dora, still shaking, looked to where Slump was pointing, and saw Pip and the other babies lined up behind the safety of the window. They were round-eyed with excitement, but not one of them was scared. "Oh," she said, and tried to stop her voice wobbling. "But what's it doing here?"

"The old ones get muddled," Slump told her as they walked into the classroom. "They see the entrance, and think they live here. It'll be off again in a minute."

"But what if it doesn't go?" Dennis wanted to know. "Do we fight it?"

Slump stared at Dennis. "I thought roofies were all mimsy wimsy stay at homes," he said. "What's with all this fighting stuff? And no. Wabbits are OK. We just have to keep clear in case they squash us by mistake."

Peg felt it was time she got a word in. "Like daft Daffy said. They're BIG."

Before the outraged Daffodil could reply, the door opened.

"Come inside, dears," Mrs Gage said. "Leave the poor wabbit to find its way out again."

"I'm NOT daft!" Daffodil hissed as she sat down at her desk.

"And I'm not a bully!" Peg hissed back. "Just wait until after school! You're DEAD!"

"Oh, yeah?" said Daffodil. "Just try!"

The rest of the day passed quickly. The rabbit, finding no trace of his friends and relations, decided to look elsewhere, and the school was briefly plunged into darkness again as he scrabbled his way out.

The playground was heaped with sandy earth after he had gone, and Mrs Gage organised a sweeping party for the afternoon's activity.

"Do wabbits come in a lot?" Dora asked Violet as they trotted around with their brooms. She was still feeling anxious.

Violet shook her head. "That's the first for AGES," she said. "They stopped after their burrowing tunnels were blocked off – well, except for the silly ones."

"Oh," Dora said. "Who blocked off the tunnels?"

Violet shuddered. "Human Beanies. They used to chase the wabbits."

Dennis heard Violet, and swaggered up to her. "We've seen Human Beanies!" he boasted.

"Were they very scary?" Violet asked.

"Yes," Dora said. "They were horrible!"

"What's that?" It was Peg. "Who's horrible?" She sniggered nastily. "We all know Violet's horrible, don't we, Vi? Horrible little flower. Should have been called Weed, shouldn't you, Vi?"

Violet cringed, and crept away.

Dennis turned on Peg. "Actually," he said, "we were talking about Human Beanies. Not that it's any of your business."

Peg's eyes narrowed. "Watch it, roofie!" she growled.

"Watch what?" Dennis asked. "Watch you picking on Violet? Why don't you pick on someone your own size?"

Peg went purple with fury, and swung her broom at Dennis. Dennis ducked, and Peg hit Plotter instead.

Plotter went flying, and cannoned into Button, who screamed and fell on top of Kittle. Kittle tried to save herself by clutching at Dora, who slid sideways, and was only saved from falling by Slump catching her arm. Violet took one look at the mayhem and ran shrieking to fetch Mrs Gage. As she disappeared into the school Daffodil grabbed Dennis, and whispered urgently into his ear.

CHAPTER SEVEN

As Dennis listened, his eyes grew wider and wider, and a smile spread over his face. He glanced at the purple and furious Peg, and nodded. "YES!" he said. "THAT'LL teach her!"

By the time Mrs Gage came hurrying into the playground more than half her pupils were picking themselves up and dusting themselves down. Danny and Sam were the only two still sweeping as if nothing had happened.

"Everybody inside NOW!" Mrs Gage snapped. She folded her arms, a grim look on her face. "Everybody inside, and sit down QUIETLY at your desks!"

The Wabbit End draglins trailed back into the classroom, Plotter rubbing his head. Peg pushed forward so she was beside Dennis, and muttered, "I'll get you for that, roofie!"

"Just you try!" Dennis told her. "I'll be waiting for you!"

Sam and Danny looked at each other, and Sam rolled his eyes. "Hope your brother's a tough kid," he said under his breath. "Peg's as mean as they come, and she doesn't fight fair."

Danny nodded wearily. He was beginning to think school was going to be extremely hard work. Why couldn't Dennis and Daffodil try and fit in for once?

Dora was thinking much the same thing. Daffodil was sitting at her desk with the most suspicious sparkle in her eyes, and Dora, who knew her well, feared the worst.

When Violet asked if Dora would like to go home with her for tea Dora apologetically said she was sorry, but she absolutely couldn't.

"I think my sister might need me," she explained.

"She doesn't look as if she needs anyone," Violet said.

"I know," Dora agreed. "But I ought to make sure she gets home safely."

Violet looked at her in wonder. "So come home with me! Then you won't have to bother about her."

Dora was shocked. "But I HAVE to bother about her," she said. "If you were in trouble, I'd stick with you too. That's what friends do, isn't it?" She stopped so she could consider what she was saying. "At least, I think that's right. I've only ever had my brothers and sister as my friends up to now, but we always do everything together." She sighed. "Even though I don't want to, sometimes."

"Oh." Violet nodded. "I see." She patted Dora's arm. "I'm glad you're my friend." She hesitated. "So should I come home with you? To make sure you're safe?"

"It's OK," Dora said. "There'll be the four of us. But thank you."

And she and Violet smiled at each other as the bell rang for the end of school.

The bell had hardly finished ringing before Daffodil was out of her desk and heading for the door. Dennis was close behind her.

Mrs Gage, who had lost a good deal of her briskness, had to stand in their way to stop them. "Just one minute, IF you please!"

Daffodil made a face, but stayed where she was. So did Dennis.

"Tomorrow," Mrs Gage said, "I would like everyone to make a brand new start. We will forget about everything that's happened today, and begin again. We will all –" she paused, and looked round meaningfully, "– ALL be friends, and be a happy family together. Is that understood?"

There were murmurs of "Yes, Mrs Gage."

Slump put up his hand. "Please, Miss," he said, "will I get to do my bootball kicking demo tomorrow?"

"I think that would be an excellent idea," Mrs Gage said. "We'll begin with bootball for everyone. And now you may go."

CHAPTER EIGHT

As Daffodil and Dennis disappeared in a cloud of dust, the rest of the class tidied their chairs, collected their lunch boxes and scurried away.

At the back of the school was a wide tunnel, part of the old burrowing, and eventually this met up with another branch of the Underground. Daffodil, Dennis, Dora, Danny and Pip were the only draglins who lived on the far side of the school; all the other little draglins took this route home.

Peg, a determined look on her face, slammed her desk lid shut and stomped off after them. She marched past the school windows so that anyone who happened to be looking out could see which way she was going; it was only when she reached the edge of the burrowing that she doubled back, and tiptoed in the other direction.

Dora, distracted by having to find both Dennis and Daffodil's lunch boxes as well as her own, was about to leave when she remembered Pip.

"Oh, bother!" she thought, and then, "That's typical of Daffy to forget him. She always forgets everything Uncle Puddle tells her." She turned, and went back through the classroom to the nursery.

To her surprise she found Danny already there. He was talking to Slump, and they were both admiring Pip's huge lump of clay. There were two sticks stuck in the top, and Pip was glowing with pride.

"Wabbit," he said when he saw Dora. "BIG wabbit."

"It's a lovely wabbit," Dora said. "Erm – do we have to take it home?"

"Of course you do," Slump told her. He pointed at another baby draglin clutching two twigs and a leaf. "My sister gets really upset if I don't bring her stuff back."

"She's sweet." Dora waved at the baby, who smiled and waved back.

Danny took Pip's hand, and handed Dora the clay rabbit wrapped in a piece of plastic bag.

Dora, already juggling three lunch boxes, managed to balance it on top of the pile.

"Come on, Dor," Danny said. "We'd better be going. Bye, Slump!"

"Cheers!" Slump gave Danny and Dora a thumbs-up. "See you tomorrow."

"Yes..." Dora hesitated. "About your boots," she said. "I really am sorry."

Slump grinned. "No probs. Just make sure you watch me kick the best goal ever tomorrow!"

"Oh – I will!" Dora promised.

"Let's hope Dennis and Daffodil are in the Underground," Danny said as they left the empty playground.

"They wouldn't go home without us, would they?" Dora asked anxiously.

Pip swung on Danny's hand. "Home!" he echoed. "Go home NOW!"

Danny shrugged. "Daffy told me to get Pip for her. My guess is they were planning some revenge on Peg."

"WHAT?" Dora stared at him in horror. "And you let them go without us? Danny – how COULD you?"

"It's OK," Danny said. "Don't flap! She went the other way. I saw her."

"Oh." Dora heaved a sigh of relief. "Let's go and find the others."

Danny was right. Daffodil had planned the revenge, and Dennis had added details.

One. A quick dash away, and into the Underground.

Two. A zoom to the clay pit, and the acquisition of several handfuls of extremely wet and sticky clay, to be hidden some way in from the Underground entrance, where the tunnel turned a sharp corner.

Three. The arrival of Peg, to be followed by a talk on the subject of bullying (Dennis's

idea) and –

Four. The delivery of the clay if all did not go well (Daffodil's idea).

So far all had gone exactly to plan; the clay was in position, and the mud-spattered Daffodil and Dennis were lurking deep in the shadows…but where was Peg?

"I'm sure she meant to follow us," Daffodil whispered.

"Maybe she changed her mind," Dennis suggested.

Daffodil frowned. "I'll be even madder with her if she has!"

Dennis rubbed his nose, leaving yet another smear. "What about Dora and Danny and Pip? They'll be along here soon."

Daffodil dismissed this with a wave of her hand. "They'll be ages yet. Pip takes FOREVER to get anywhere."

"We'll just have to wait and see who gets here first," Dennis said, and sat down.

"OK," Daffodil said, and sat down beside him.

CHAPTER NINE

Outside the entrance to the Underground Dora was trying to balance three lunch boxes and an enormous lump of slippery clay that kept threatening to escape from its plastic wrapping. It didn't help that Pip was insisting he carried it himself.

"Why don't you just let him take it?" Danny said. "He'll soon give it back. It weighs a ton."

"WABBIT!" Pip demanded.

"He'll get filthy," Dora said.

"It'll wash off," Danny said.

"DO stop fussing, Dor. We'll NEVER get home at this rate, and I'm STARVING!"

Dora sighed, and handed Pip the lump of clay. "WABBIT!" Pip said proudly, and clutched it tightly to his chest as the three of them went through the opening...and a fiercely scowling Peg stepped out in front of them.

Dora's legs turned to jelly, and her heart thumped wildly.

"Why – if it isn't know-it-all Dora and her ickle pickle baby brother!" Peg said, with a nasty leer at Pip.

Danny swallowed hard. "Just let us take Pip home," he said. "You can fight us another time, but not now. We don't want trouble."

"Ooooh!" Peg sneered. "Who's trying to be a big brave brother? Well, I'm going to teach you two a lesson, so Big Head Dennis and Big Mouth Daffy-waffy will know I mean what I say!" And she stepped forward – just as Pip dropped his massive lump of clay, and yelled "WABBIT!" at the top of his squeaky little voice... and everything was swallowed up in darkness.

When Dora was telling Violet what happened the next day, she found she couldn't remember what happened in which order.

Possibly Peg, taken completely by surprise, tripped on the clay and fell flat on her face and then it went dark – or perhaps everything went completely black, and then Peg fell over. At any rate, it was impossible to see anything; all that could be heard were thumps and shouts and scufflings, and Pip yelling, "See wabbit! See wabbit NOW!"

The light was very very tiny at first; a minute star twinkling in the black night of the burrow. Gradually it came closer, and the thumps and shouts and scuffles stopped.

"What's that light, Daffy?" asked Dennis's voice.

"Don't know," Daffodil answered, and Dora, crouching down with her arms round Pip, sighed in relief.

"It's coming closer," Danny said.

A moment later they saw it was Mrs Gage, holding a lantern. "Don't be frightened," she said. "It's that wabbit again…" and the rabbit fell into the burrowing, bringing light and air with its fall.

Mrs Gage and the little draglins blinked, and an ecstatic Pip crowed with excitement. Mrs Gage wasn't interested in the rabbit. She was looking at Peg, flat on her face, and covered in splats of yellow clay. Dennis, Danny and Daffodil were standing round her, covered in mud from head to foot, but attempting to look the picture of innocence.

Dora was doing her best to stop Pip from rushing to pat the rabbit's paws.

Before Mrs Gage could speak, Peg heaved herself up and onto her excessively muddy feet. She looked down at her clothes and her shoes, and to the draglins' amazement an expression of total horror came over her face. "Oh NO!" she gasped. "My mum will KILL me!"

"But whatever's happened to you?" Mrs Gage asked. "What's been going on here?"

Peg and Daffodil looked at each other for a long moment.

"Well?" Mrs Gage raised her eyebrows.

"Poor Peg slipped on Pip's clay rabbit," Daffodil said quickly. "It was all my fault."

"It was my fault too," Dennis chipped in.

"Actually, it was more mine," Danny said. "I was looking after Pip."

"And I was," Dora said.

"Wabbit," Pip said, still gazing at his hero, who was sitting in the middle of the school playground cleaning his paws.

Peg wiped the mud out of her ears. "Should have looked where I was going," she said gruffly. "See you guys tomorrow." And she began to stamp away.

Dora jumped to her feet. If there was one thing she recognised, and sympathised with, it was desperation. Especially when combined with terror.

"Peg," she said, "why don't you come home with us? Aunt Plum's BRILLIANT at cleaning and washing. You can have tea with us, and a wash before you go home..."

Her voice died away. Peg was staring at her with the most peculiar expression. Dora gave up. "I just thought it might help..." she mumbled.

Peg burst into tears. She sobbed and sobbed, and her shoulders heaved, and she sobbed some more, then wailed, "I was going to beat you up! And you're being NICE to me!"

"Oh, PEG!" Mrs Gage said helplessly.

Dora fished a snow-white hanky out of her pocket. She handed it to Peg. "Here you are," she said. "And now I do think we'd better be going. Aunt Plum and the uncles will be wondering where we are."

"Yeah." Daffodil grinned at Peg. "Come and meet the uncles!"

Peg blew her nose hard. "OK."

"NO," Pip said. "See wabbit!"

"The wabbit will be going to bed soon," Dora told him. "Let's go home, and I'll push you on the swing."

"SWING!" Pip rushed into the Underground, and Dora hurried after him.

As Peg followed Dora, Daffodil, Dennis, Danny and Pip, Mrs Gage noticed that the clay plastered over her back was covered in little hand prints.

"H'm," she said to herself, and then, "but they're all friends now. And it could be a trick of the light."

Behind her the rabbit finished cleaning itself, and hopped towards the way out.

Mrs Gage shook her head. "Tomorrow," she told the rabbit, "I shall ask Mr Puddle and Mr Plant if they can find some way of making that burrowing MUCH narrower." And she sat down to wait for the rabbit to leave.

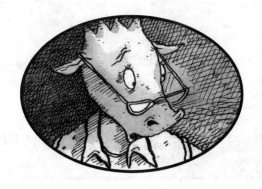

CHAPTER TEN

Aunt Plum, Uncle Damson, Uncle Plant and Uncle Puddle stared as the procession of draglins trotted out of the Underground and across to the front gate of Under Roof. Pip was in front, and he was moderately muddy. Dora was next, and she was, for Dora, remarkably muddy.

Dennis, Daffodil and Danny were almost unrecognisable, and behind them was a figure who seemed to be mud from top to bottom.

Aunt Plum thought of her gleaming floors, and groaned.

Uncle Puddle decided that this was the moment to use the garden hose that he had spent many hours constructing from a handful of Collected drinking straws.

Uncle Plant and Uncle Damson stood and blinked.

Daffodil put on a sudden spurt, and arrived first. "Hey!" she said, and her smile was dazzling. "School's BRILLIANT! We've brought Peg back for tea – is that OK? Oh, she might need a bit of a wash, but Dora told her you're the best EVER at cleaning, Aunt Plum."

"Thank you, Daffodil dear," Aunt Plum said faintly. She looked at Dora. "Did you enjoy yourself, Dora?"

Dora nodded. "Yes, thank you, Aunt Plum." She saw her aunt's face, and added, "We're very sorry about the mess. Pip made a clay wabbit, and the clay sort of got everywhere."

"Wabbit," Pip agreed.

"Come on, Peg," Daffodil said. "I'll show you my beetle!"

"DON'T GO THROUGH THE HOUSE!" Aunt Plum wailed...but she was too late.

There was a pause. Danny looked at his speechless uncles, and squinted up at the sun. "We're back on time," he said cheerfully. "So THAT'S good, isn't it?"

"Yes," Dennis said. "Can't wait for tomorrow, can we, Danny?"

"No," Danny said. "Come on, Dor. Let's go and see what Peg and Daffy are up to..."

"Coming," Dora said, and she smiled happily. "Tomorrow I'm going to watch Slump play bootball, Aunt Plum. Isn't that GREAT?" And she hurried away.

by Vivian French
illustrated by Chris Fisher

All priced at £3.99.

Draglins books are available from all good bookshops,
or can be ordered direct from the publisher:
Orchard Books, PO BOX 29, Douglas IM99 1BQ.
Credit card orders please telephone 01624 836000
or fax 01624 837033 or visit our website:
www.orchardbooks.co.uk
or e-mail: bookshop@enterprise.net for details.

To order please quote title, author and ISBN
and your full name and address.
Cheques and postal orders should be made
payable to 'Bookpost plc.'

Postage and packing is FREE within the UK
(overseas customers should add £2.00 per book).

Prices and availability are subject to change.